ALL MY
SHINING
SILVER

Dorling **DK** Kindersley

LONDON, NEW YORK, SYDNEY, DELHI, PARIS
MUNICH and JOHANNESBURG

*For Amelia Elise Muenzberg
and Alexandra Nicole Muenzberg*

Project Editor Fiona Munro
Designer Sarah Crouch
Senior Editor Marie Greenwood
Managing Art Editor Jacquie Gulliver
Production Jo Rooke, Nicola Torode

First American Edition, 2000
00 01 02 03 04 05 10 9 7 6 5 4 3 2 1

Published in the United States by
Dorling Kindersley Publishing, Inc.
95 Madison Avenue
New York, New York 10016

Library of Congress Cataloging-in-Publication Data
Baumgartner, Barbara.
    All my shining silver : stories of values from around the world / retold by Barbara Baumgartner ; illustrated
by Amanda Hall.--1st American ed.
    p. cm.
Contents: All my shining silver (Ireland) -- Awang and his silver flute (Indonesia) -- Hadiyah and the great fish
(Mozambique) -- The danced-out shoes (Russia) -- Why dog and cat are not friends (Japan and Korea) -- The
rainbow horse (Puerto Rico)
    ISBN 0-7894-6663-5
    1. Tales. [1. Folklore.] I. Hall, Amanda, ill. II. Title.

PZ8.1.B345 Al 2000
398.2--dc21
                                    00-022671

Color reproduction by DOT Gradations

Printed in China by L. Rex

see our complete
catalog at
www.dk.com

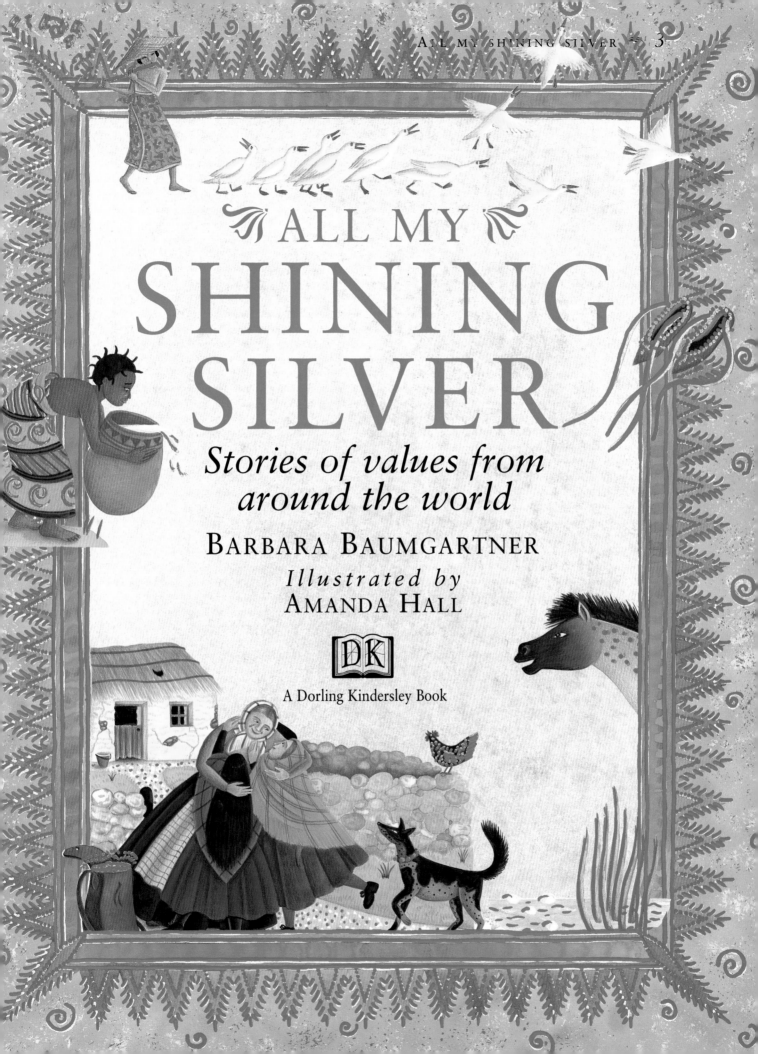

ALL MY SHINING SILVER

Stories of values from around the world

BARBARA BAUMGARTNER

Illustrated by
AMANDA HALL

DK

A Dorling Kindersley Book

Introduction
A note for parents and teachers

In many ways, television and computers isolate us from face-to-face interactions with other people. By way of contrast, storytelling and reading aloud in the home and in the classroom demonstrate and promote interpersonal communication. As you read these stories aloud, or tell them in your own words, the eye contact you make gives each listener the sense that you are her own personal storyteller.

Old stories, such as the ones I have retold for this book, hold deep wisdom about the ideals of human behavior. Children who hear the stories often continue to reflect on them, as they are walking home from school or falling asleep at night. Even though a moral is printed at the end of each story, ask the children what they think is important about a tale, and they will share their own unique insights.

So, tell the stories, and make them come alive!

Contents

All My Shining Silver ➤

AN IRISH FOLKTALE

ONCE THERE WAS a mother who had two daughters. When her husband died, he had left her a long leather bag full of shining silver coins. The mother thought they would always have money for food and clothes.

But one day a strange old woman came begging at the door. She was bent over with age and her long straggly white hair flew out in every direction. The girls' mother knew it could bring bad luck if she did not feed the woman, so she invited her in and served her bread and tea.

But the next day the mother realized that the long leather bag was gone – the strange old woman must have stolen it, and now she was far away.

From that day on, the mother had a hard time raising her two daughters.

If there was a leak in the thatched roof, she had no money to fix it. Sometimes there was a poor crop of potatoes, and they did not have enough to eat.

One day Maureen, the older daughter, said "Mother, I'm old enough to find a job. Bake me a bannock and I'll go to seek my fortune."

The mother baked her a bannock, which looked like a big, flat biscuit. Then she said, "Maureen, will you take half the bannock with my blessing, or the whole bannock without?"

Maureen answered, "Well Mother, I'd rather have the whole bannock without your blessing. If I'm not back home in a year and a day, you will know that I am earning money and living well."

So Maureen set out, right foot, left foot, walking down the road. Now and then she would stop and knock at the door of a farmhouse to ask for work. But she always got the same answer, "Well, Miss, we've plenty of workers here and hardly enough food to feed them all. You'll have to look somewhere else."

Finally, Maureen knocked at the door of a little old house. An old woman, all bent over with straggly white hair, answered the door.

"I'm looking for work," said the girl.

"You can work for me," said the old woman. "You must wash the clothes, cook the food, and sweep the hearth. But you must never look up the chimney, or you'll have bad luck!"

Maureen agreed, and she began to work for the old woman.

Every morning, Maureen got up early and cooked breakfast. Then she washed the dishes and swept the hearth. After the old woman had gone out, Maureen cooked soup for lunch.

One day she thought, *It won't hurt if I look up the chimney*. But when she did, she saw her own mother's long leather bag. Maureen grabbed the leather bag and started to run home as fast as she could.

Soon she came to a horse grazing in a field.
The horse called out,

"Rub me! Rub me!
I haven't been rubbed
For seven years!"

Maureen yelled, "Get out of my way, you stupid horse,"
and she ran on and on.
Soon she came to a sheep. The sheep called out,

"Shear me! Shear me!
I haven't been shorn
For seven years!"

But Maureen said, "Get out of my way, you stupid
sheep," and she ran on and on.
By now it was late in the day. When she came
to a mill, the mill wheel
cried out,

"Turn me! Turn me!
I haven't been turned
For seven years!"

But Maureen said, "Not you, too! I'm so tired of
being asked to do things!"
Then she went inside the mill and lay down behind
the door, with the long leather bag under her head. Soon
she fell asleep.

Now, when the old woman came back to her hut, she saw that Maureen was gone. She ran to the chimney and looked up. The long leather bag was gone, too. The old woman ran out of the door and down the road. When she came to the horse, she called out,

"Horse, horse of mine
Where's that maid of mine,
With a wig and a wag,
With a long leather bag
And all my shining silver?"

"Oh," said the horse, "she ran past not long ago."
The old woman ran until she came to the sheep.

"Sheep, sheep of mine
Where's that maid of mine,
With a wig and a wag,
With a long leather bag
And all my shining silver?"

"Oh," said the sheep, "she ran past not long ago."
The old woman ran until she came to the mill.

"Mill, mill of mine
Where's that maid of mine,
With a wig and a wag,
With a long leather bag
And all my shining silver?"

The mill said, "She is behind the door." So
the old woman went in and smacked the girl
with her walking stick – which turned the girl into stone.
Then she picked up the long leather bag and went home.

Now a year and a day went by after Maureen left home. The younger sister, Kate, said, "Mother, my sister must be earning a great fortune. If I go and look for a job, you'll have one less mouth to feed, and I may find my fortune."

The mother baked her a bannock. Then she said, "Kate, will you take half the bannock with my blessing, or the whole bannock without?"

Kate answered, "Mother, I'd rather have your blessing and half the bannock." So her mother gave her a blessing and half the bannock.

Kate started walking down the road. Now and then she knocked at a farmhouse to ask for work. But she always got the same answer, "Well, Miss, we have plenty of workers here and hardly enough to feed them. You'll have to look somewhere else."

Finally, Kate knocked at the door of a little old house. An old woman, all bent over with straggly white hair, answered the door.

"I've come to find work," said the girl.

"You can work for me," said the old woman. "You must wash the clothes, cook the food, and sweep the hearth. But you must never look up the chimney, or you'll have bad luck!"

Kate agreed and she began working. The next morning, Kate got up early and cooked breakfast. Then she washed the dishes and swept the hearth. After the old woman had gone out, Kate cooked soup for lunch. Then she thought, *It won't hurt if I look up the chimney.*

But when she did, she saw her mother's own leather bag, full of shining silver. Kate grabbed the bag and started to run home as fast she could.

Soon she came to a horse grazing in a field. The horse called out,

"Rub me! Rub me!
I haven't been rubbed
For seven years!"

Kate said, "Oh, you poor horse. I will rub you." Then she grabbed a handful of grass, and rubbed the horse all over. Soon she came to a sheep. The sheep called out,

"Shear me! Shear me!
I haven't been shorn
For seven years!"

Kate said, "Oh, you poor sheep. I will help you." Then she took a pair of shears that were hanging on the fence and cut the sheep's wool. Then Kate ran on and on. It was late in the day when she came to a mill. The mill wheel called out,

"Turn me! Turn me!
I haven't been turned
For seven years!"

Kate said, "Oh, poor mill, I will turn your wheel." And she did. Soon it was dark, so Kate went into the mill and lay down behind the door, with the long leather bag under her head. Then she fell asleep.

When the old woman came back to her hut, she saw that Kate was gone. She ran to the chimney and looked up. The long leather bag was gone, too. The old woman ran out of the door and down the road.

When she came to the horse, she called out,

"Horse, horse of mine
Where's that maid of mine,
With a wig and a wag,
With a long leather bag
And all my shining silver?"

The horse said, "Do you think I have time to
watch your maids for you? Go and look for her yourself."
The old woman ran on until she came to the sheep.

"Sheep, sheep of mine
Where's that maid of mine,
With a wig and a wag,
With a long leather bag
And all my shining silver?"

The sheep said, "Do you think I have time to watch your maids
for you? Go and look for her yourself."
The old woman ran on until she came to the mill.

"Mill, mill of mine
Where's that maid of mine,
With a wig and a wag,
With a long leather bag
And all my shining silver?"

The mill said, "Do you think I have time to watch your maids
for you? Go and look for her yourself."

The old woman swore at the mill, and the mill wheel tripped her so that she fell and dropped her walking stick. Then the mill door swung closed with a terrible screeching sound, locking the old woman out. She was so frightened by the mill wheel tripping her and the mill door closing on her that she ran off and was never seen again.

The next morning, the mill wheel told Kate to pick up the old woman's walking stick and touch it to the stone lying behind the door. When she did, up jumped her sister Maureen, alive and well. Kate picked up the long leather bag, and the two of them walked home.

Their mother was glad to see them. She had been sad the whole time they were gone. And so they lived well and happy for the rest of their days, with all their shining silver.

HELPING OTHERS BRINGS ITS OWN REWARDS!

Hadiyah and the Great Fish 〜
A FOLKTALE FROM MOZAMBIQUE

*L*ong ago the people who lived near the Zambezi River believed that the river was guarded by a Great Spirit in the shape of a silver-scaled fish. In that long-ago time, Hadiyah lived with her mother and her little sister, Imani. Hadiyah was tall and graceful, but the Chief's daughter, Layla, was jealous and led the other girls in teasing and making fun of her. "Hadiyah, you hold your head high, but you are not as important as I am!"

Often the girls of the village went to the riverbank to dig clay, which they would use to plaster the walls of their huts. One day Layla said, "Hadiyah, it is your turn to climb down into the clay pit."

Hadiyah wanted to be helpful, so she climbed down into the pit. Three sides of the pit were clay earth, while the fourth side opened into the river. Hadiyah used a digging stick to scrape lumps of clay, which she then handed up to Layla. As Hadiyah worked, she could feel the river water lapping at her ankles.

When Layla's basket was full, she said, "Well, I have all I need, Hadiyah. I'm going home." And she and her friends hurried off, laughing cruelly at Hadiyah's predicament.

There was no one to help Hadiyah climb out of the pit, and the river was rising quickly from the recent rains. Hadiyah was scared and didn't know what to do. When she saw the Great Fish swimming toward her, she thought that it might help her. The magical silver-scaled fish said to her, "Step into my mouth, and I will keep you safe from harm."

As Hadiyah stepped inside the mouth of the Great Fish, it was as if she had entered a land of peace. She saw people hoeing vegetables, and heard them singing as they worked.

She felt a sense of calm and safety, not the panic she had felt while she was trapped in the clay pit. That evening, when Hadiyah did not return home, her mother was worried. She went to the nightly gathering, where all the villagers sat around the campfire to tell the news of the day and listen to the elders tell stories of long ago. This night, Hadiyah's mother said, "Hadiyah did not return from digging clay today. Has anyone seen her?" No one spoke. Several of the men said they would search for Hadiyah, and they left the campfire.

But the next night the searchers reported that they had not found Hadiyah, alive or dead. Now the whole village wept for Hadiyah. They were sure they would never see her again.

Meanwhile, Hadiyah had only the faintest memory of her mother and sister, until one afternoon when she heard the sound of Imani crying. She said to the Great Fish, "I must go and help my sister. I hear her crying."

The Great Fish replied, "Go, but come back. If a person from the earth world touches you now, you will die."

Hadiyah stepped out of the river, moving slowly, as one does who is under an enchantment. Her arms and legs were covered with silver fish scales. As she walked toward the shore, she could see what had happened. Since she herself was not at home, her mother had sent Imani with the older girls to fetch water from the river. Even now, Hadiyah could see the older girls laughing as they walked toward the village, each of them balancing her water jug on her head. Little Imani still stood at the river's edge, crying as she struggled to lift the full water jug. Hadiyah silently stepped forward. "Imani," she said, "do not touch me and do not tell anyone that you have seen me." Hadiyah lifted the water jug and walked part of the way to the village. Then she balanced the jug on Imani's head, turned and glided back into the river. This happened each time that Imani came to fetch water, but Imani never told anyone that she had seen Hadiyah.

Then one day Imani's mother said, "Imani, take this jug of ale to the Chief." Imani said, in her small voice, "Mama, it is too heavy for me to lift by myself."

Her mother said, "How do you lift the full water jug at the river?"

"Hadiyah helps me."

Her mother wondered at that, so the next day when Imani went to get water from the river with the older girls, her mother followed a little way behind, hiding among the trees. As she watched, she saw all the village girls fill their water jugs and start home while Imani was still filling her jug. Then she saw Hadiyah step out of the river. Hadiyah's arms and legs were covered with silver fish scales. She moved slowly, as if she were in a dream. Hadiyah lifted the water jug and walked beside Imani. Then the mother stepped out onto the path.

Hadiyah gasped, "Oh, Mother, do not touch me. I cannot come home just yet." After Hadiyah helped Imani balance the water jug on her head, she turned and glided back into the river.

That night, at the village gathering, Hadiyah's mother said, "On the day that Hadiyah disappeared, who else went digging?"

Several of the girls began to squirm with embarrassment and one of them said, "Layla made fun of Hadiyah and left her in the clay pit."

Layla's grandmother asked, "Layla, what do you have to say for yourself?"

Layla complained, "Hadiyah always held her head high, as if she were proud of herself and thought she was better than I who am the Chief's daughter!"

The grandmother said, "But Layla, how would you have felt if Hadiyah had left you to drown in the clay pit?"

Layla shivered at the thought of being drowned, then hung her head in shame. "I did not think of that."

Another girl said, "But you are also mean to Imani! You do not help her lift the water jug onto her head."

Layla said softly, "I can try to be nicer. I can treat Imani as if she were my own little sister."

About this time, Hadiyah felt a great longing to return to the land of the living. She spoke to the Great Fish, saying, "Great Fish, you have helped me when I was in deep trouble, but now I want to return to the land of the living, to be with my mother and sister."

The Great Fish was silent for a moment. Then he said, "You have my permission to go. But take this magic wand with you. When you stand in the doorway of your mother's hut, touch it to the silver scales on your arms and legs. Then you will be human again."

The next day at sunset, Hadiyah stood in the doorway of her mother's hut. In her hand she carried the magic wand. She said, "Mother, I have come home." Then she touched the magic wand to her arms and legs. All the shining silver scales fell off, and turned into silver coins.

Hadiyah's mother used the silver coins to have a festival, and the whole village, even Layla, celebrated Hadiyah's return.

BE A FRIEND,
NOT A RIVAL

Awang and His Silver Flute

AN OLD STORY FROM INDONESIA

Long ago in Indonesia there lived a boy named Awang. His mother told him to take the ducks to the market and sell them. As Awang started walking to market, driving his ducks before him, he began playing his silver flute and daydreaming.

I have so many ducks!

You will hear my ducks upstream: pak, pak, pak.

You will hear my ducks downstream: pak, pak, pak.

My ducks will eat the rice in the fields.

My cousins will say, "Whose ducks are these?"

My mother will answer, "These are Awang's ducks!"

Awang continued playing his flute and daydreaming.

I will sell the ducks and buy many goats.
You will hear my goats upstream: maa, maa, maa.
You will hear my goats downstream: maa, maa, maa.
My goats will eat the crops.
My cousins will say, "Whose goats are these?"
My mother will answer, "These are Awang's goats."
Then I will sell the goats and buy many elephants.
You will hear my elephants upstream: ruh, ruh, ruh.
You will hear my elephants downstream: ruh, ruh, ruh.
My elephants will pull up the trees.
My elephants will come into the village and knock over the houses.

"Stop!" shouted Awang out loud. "The elephants are trampling my mother's house!" He began swinging his silver flute as if it were a sword and the ducks ran away in fright.

Now Awang walked along, no ducks, no goats, no elephants. But he began playing his silver flute again. Then he thought to himself,
        The trees ask, "Whose flute is this?"
        And the wind will answer,
        "This is Awang's flute!"

DON'T CONFUSE DREAMS
WITH REAL LIFE

The Danced-Out Shoes ᕥ

AN OLD STORY FROM RUSSIA

Once there was a King who had three daughters.
Elena was skillful at playing the piano,
Marissa could sew and embroider shirts and blouses,
and Natasha baked delicious breads and cakes.

But the King had a problem. Every morning his daughters asked him to
buy them new shoes. But the following morning the new shoes were lying
beside their beds, all tattered and torn. The King wondered what his
daughters did each night to wear out their shoes, but they would not tell him.

One day, the King announced that he would give a bag of silver coins to any man who could discover how the princesses wore out their shoes every night.

For a whole year, one young man after another came to the palace to try to solve the riddle of the danced-out shoes. But each, in turn, ended up falling asleep, and each, in turn, was sent away.

One day, a soldier traveled to the palace. On the way, he met an old woman who asked where he was going.

He said, "I would like to find out where the princesses dance away the night, but I'm afraid I'll fail like all the others."

The old woman said, "I will tell you one thing not to do and one thing to do: you must not drink the sleeping potion that the eldest princess offers you; and you must pretend to be asleep."

"That sounds easy enough," said the soldier.

She gave him a cloak that was as light as a feather. "This will make you invisible. When the princesses leave their bedroom, put on the cloak and follow them."

The soldier thanked the old woman and walked up to the castle, where he was greeted kindly. That evening, after supper, a servant showed him to the room next to the princesses' bedroom. Elena brought him a silver cup containing wine and a sleeping potion. The soldier thanked her and took the cup. But he only pretended to drink. Then he lay down on the bed and soon began snoring loudly, as if he were asleep. He listened carefully to hear what the princesses would say and do.

Marissa laughed, saying,

"He is as foolish as all the others. Now we can go dancing."

When the soldier heard this, he put on his invisible cape and tiptoed into their room. The three sisters were already wearing their dancing dresses and their new dancing shoes.

Then Elena went to the foot of her bed and lifted it up. Then she, Marissa and Natasha began descending a spiral staircase with silver railings. The soldier quickly followed Natasha. When he accidentally stepped on the hem of her dress, Natasha cried out, "Sisters, someone stepped on my hem! That soldier must be following us!"

"Silly goose," said Elena. "Your hem caught on a nail."

When they reached the bottom of the stairs, they entered an underground kingdom, where all the trees had silver leaves. The soldier thought, *If I take a silver twig with me, I can prove to the King that I was here.* He reached up and snapped off a twig.

Natasha jumped with fright and said, "Something is wrong! Did you hear that cracking sound?"

"Don't be so jumpy," said Marissa. "Listen! You can hear the music playing in the palace of the Fairy King!"

Soon they reached the underground palace, and each sister began dancing. They danced and danced till their shoes were all tattered and torn.

When a servant passed out silver cups of wine, each of the sisters took one. The soldier, still invisible in his cloak, also took a silver cup. He poured the wine away, then hid the silver cup in the folds of his cloak.

When the dance was over, the princesses said goodnight to their partners, and hurried through the silver wood. As soon as they got to their own bedroom, they took off their danced-out shoes and fell asleep.

The soldier slipped invisibly into his own room.

The next morning, the King asked the soldier, "Have you solved the riddle? Do you know how my daughters wear out their shoes every night?"

The soldier said, "They go to the underground palace of the Fairy King, and there they dance all night. I have brought some things from that underground kingdom."

The King called his daughters into the room and said, "This soldier can prove that you dance the night away in the palace of the Fairy King."

"Father," said Elena, "he cannot offer proof. He slept like a log all night."

The soldier took the silver twig out of his left pocket and the silver cup out of his right pocket. "This should be proof enough," he said.

Natasha gasped, "Oh, I thought I heard a twig snap as we walked through the forest."

The King said, "But why do you creep away every night?"

Marissa said, "Father, you won't let us have a party. We love to dance!"

The King said, "Let us compromise. Once a week you may invite friends here to dance. But you must agree that you will never creep away again."

Elena, Marissa, and Natasha agreed and the King rewarded the soldier with a bag of silver coins. The King and his daughters kept their agreements, and they lived in peace and happiness the rest of their days.

USE YOUR WITS TO GAIN YOUR FORTUNE

The Rainbow Horse

AN OLD TALE FROM PUERTO RICO

L ong ago in Puerto Rico, there lived a farmer and his three sons, Carlos, Pedro, and Juan. One morning the farmer said, "Last night a wild animal ate some of our corn."

Carlos said, "Tonight, father, I will catch that wild animal. I'll borrow the hammock and take a rope to lasso the creature."

His father agreed, and at sunset, Carlos went to the field and strung the hammock between two trees nearby. Then he sat down in the hammock to wait, but soon he fell asleep.

When Carlos awoke the next morning, he saw that the wild animal had again eaten some of the corn.

So Carlos went home, feeling annoyed that he had failed.

Then Pedro, the second son, said, "Tonight, father, I will catch the wild animal. Let me take the hammock, the rope and the guitar. I can sing songs to keep myself awake."

At sunset, Pedro took the hammock, the rope, and the guitar and walked to the cornfield. After he hung the hammock, he sat in it and began to play the guitar and sing songs. But soon he, too, fell asleep.

When Pedro awoke the next morning, he saw that the wild animal had again eaten some corn.

So Pedro went home, feeling angry that he had failed.

Then the youngest son, Juan, said, "Father, I will watch for the wild animal tonight. Let me take the hammock, the rope, the guitar, and a basket."

Carlos said, "How will you catch the wild animal?"

Pedro said, "You're not as strong as I am! Do you think you will catch it in that basket?"

At sunset, Juan took the hammock, the rope, the guitar, and the basket. As he walked toward the corn field, he picked burrs and thorns and put them in the basket.

Juan strung the hammock between the two trees, then
he stuck the thorns and prickly burrs all over it, except
for the place where he would sit.

Juan sat on the hammock and began to play the
guitar and sing songs. Each time he began to fall asleep,
he would fall against the prickly burrs and wake up.

At midnight, Juan heard the sound of a horse galloping
toward the field. He was surprised to see that the horse
shimmered with all the colors of the rainbow, and that it
had a silvery mane and tail. The horse began to trample the
corn and eat it. Quickly, Juan threw the lasso, and it
caught the little horse around the neck.

Juan called out, "Stop, Rainbow Horse. Do not trample
my father's field. Do not eat my father's corn!"

The Rainbow Horse said, "If you let me go,
I promise not to eat your father's corn again.
And if you ever need help, call me by saying:
Come, my little horse!
Come, my little Rainbow!"

Juan agreed, and he let the horse go. Then he went home and told his father that the wild animal would never again trample the fields.

But the two older brothers were jealous of Juan, so whenever their father was out working in the fields, they made him do all the work.

"Juan, wash our clothes!"

"Juan, cook our lunch!"

Juan smiled secretly to himself. They could order him around or call him nasty names, but he had a secret friend – the Rainbow Horse.

One day, the two older brothers rode into town. When they came back, they were excited.

Carlos said, "What an unusual way for the Mayor to choose a husband for his daughter, Isabella."

Pedro said, "Yes, to win her, a young man must ride his galloping horse past her balcony and toss an apple right into her hands, three days in a row."
Carlos said, "Let's try it tomorrow!"

When Carlos saw Juan listening at the door, he scolded, "Hurry up, Juan, bring us our soup."

The next day, as soon as Carlos and Pedro had left for town, Juan called,
     "Come, my little horse!
     Come, my little Rainbow!"
The horse appeared, with a silver apple in its mouth. It laid the apple
at Juan's feet and said, "Juan, would you like to toss this apple into
Isabella's hands?"
     Juan said he would, so he climbed onto the horse's back
and they galloped into town.

Juan watched as Carlos rode past the balcony where Isabella sat. Carlos tossed a shiny red apple, but it went over her head.

Then Pedro rode past, but his apple fell at her feet.

Next, the Rainbow Horse rode past the balcony, and Juan tossed the silver apple right into Isabella's outstretched hands. But instead of stopping, the horse galloped away and carried Juan home.

That evening, when the two brothers came home, they were arguing.

"I wonder who was riding on that Rainbow Horse."

"He certainly threw that silver apple well, right into Isabella's hands!"

"I wonder if he's anyone we know?"

Juan was stirring his soup and singing a little song,

"Is he friend or is he foe?

Who he is, you do not know!"

Carlos called out, "Juan, stop that mumbling and bring us our soup!"

The next day, Carlos and Pedro set out for town. As soon as they were gone, Juan called,

"Come, my little horse!

Come, my little Rainbow!"

Again, the Rainbow Horse came galloping with a silver apple in its mouth. Juan quickly climbed onto the horse's back and rode into town.

When they got there, Carlos was galloping past Isabella's balcony. This time he tossed his apple more gently, but it fell at her feet. Next came Pedro, who threw his apple so hard that it soared over Isabella's head and bounced off the wall.

Then the Rainbow Horse galloped past the balcony, and the mysterious rider tossed a silver apple right into Isabella's outstretched hands. Again the horse galloped on, carrying Juan home.

That evening, when Carlos and Pedro returned home, they were grumbling and complaining about their bad luck. Carlos said, "There were so many people, I got nervous and made a bad throw."

Pedro said, "If my saddle hadn't slipped, I would have tossed my apple correctly. That stranger is stealing our good luck!"

Carlos said, "Yes, I wonder if he's anyone we know."

Juan was stirring the soup and singing a little song,

"Is he a friend or is he a foe?
Who is he, you do not know!"

Pedro said, "Juan, stop that mumbling and bring us our soup!"

On the third day, when the two older brothers set off for town, Juan again called

"Come, my little horse!
Come, my little Rainbow!"

The horse galloped up, with a silver apple in its mouth.

In the town square, a big crowd had gathered to watch for the mysterious rider and his Rainbow Horse.

This time, Carlos threw his shiny red apple too hard, and it soared over Isabella's head, while Pedro threw his apple too softly and it landed at her feet.

As the Rainbow Horse and rider galloped past the balcony, Juan again tossed his silver apple, and, again, Isabella caught it.

This time, the Rainbow Horse stopped in front of the balcony. The Mayor came out and said, "Juan, I see that you have won the right to marry my daughter."

Carlos and Pedro ran up to Juan. They were jealous of his good fortune and asked, "Juan, how did you do that? Where did you get that horse?"

Juan told them how he had captured the horse as it was trampling their father's corn, and how it had promised that if Juan would let it go free, it would never trample the corn again, and Juan could call on it for help.

The two older brothers understood that Juan's good nature and helpfulness had enabled him to win Isabella as his bride. They felt sorry that they had been unkind to him.

On the day Juan and Isabella were married, all the people came to celebrate. Carlos and Pedro played the guitar, while everyone sang and danced.

GOOD SENSE AND A GOOD
NATURE BRING THEIR
OWN REWARDS

Why Dog and Cat are not Friends

AN OLD STORY FROM JAPAN AND KOREA

Long ago, the dog and the cat were best of friends. They lived with an old couple who were very poor. Kita wove cloth, and her husband, Taro, took it to the market to sell. Sometimes he walked through the woods to the market town in the north. On other days, he got a ride across the river to the market town in the south.

One day, Taro set out carrying a bundle of cloth under each arm. As he was walking through the woods on his way to the market, he saw a hunter aiming his gun at a monkey.

"Don't shoot!" Taro shouted, as he waved his arms. His movement startled the hunter, but the gun went off and the bullet grazed Taro's arm. He fell to the ground, with his arm bleeding. When the hunter saw what he had done, he was scared and ran away.

But the monkeys in the trees saw Taro lying on the ground. They climbed down and took care of the old man, putting healing herbs on his bleeding arm and bringing him fruit to eat.

The next day, Taro
was better. He thanked the
monkeys and started walking home.
But one of the monkeys hurried after Taro
and gave him a silver ring.

When Taro got home, his dog and cat ran to greet
him. His wife Kita said, "Oh, Taro, what happened?
You have been gone two days and now you come back
with a sore arm, still carrying the two bundles of cloth!"

Taro said, "Do not worry, Kita. I was wounded by a hunter.
But at least I stopped him from killing one of the
monkeys. The monkeys cared for me, and then they gave me
this silver ring. I will just put it in the cupboard."

So Taro set the ring on the shelf next to their last bag of
rice. That evening, when Kita was ready to
cook the rice, she opened the cupboard. "Taro!" she
called, "Come quickly! Now, instead of one bag of rice,
there are two!"

"Hmm," said Taro, "maybe this is a magic ring."
He put the ring next to Kita's comb. In the morning there
were two combs.

The next night, Taro put the magic ring in the
cupboard with his jacket. When morning came, there
were two jackets.

"I see!" said Taro. "This magic ring doubles
everything it touches."

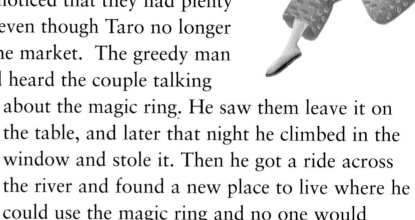

Now Kita and Taro had more than enough of everything. And there was always food for the dog and cat.

But a greedy neighbor noticed that they had plenty of food and new clothes, even though Taro no longer carried bolts of cloth to the market. The greedy man peered in the window and heard the couple talking about the magic ring. He saw them leave it on the table, and later that night he climbed in the window and stole it. Then he got a ride across the river and found a new place to live where he could use the magic ring and no one would recognize him.

Without the magic ring, Taro and Kita had many troubles. After a few days they had nothing to eat. When their clothes became worn out, there was no magic ring to help them get new ones.

One morning, Kita said, "Today, Taro, you must take this cloth and sell it in the market."

The cat and the dog decided to travel with Taro and help look for the missing ring. When Taro rode across the river with the ferryman, the cat and the dog went, too. While Taro went to the market, the cat and the dog searched. They would run into a house, look around, and run out again.

Finally, the dog found the magic silver ring under a pillow in the greedy man's house. He carried it in his mouth, and he soon found the cat. The two of them ran to the river, but they could not see Taro or the ferryman.

The dog laid the ring on the ground and said, "Cat, I will swim across the river. You can ride on my back and carry the ring in your mouth." The cat agreed.

The dog began to swim across the river, with the cat clinging to his back. Halfway across, the dog asked, "Is the ring all right?"

The cat held the ring tightly in her mouth and could not answer. As they got closer to the bank, the dog barked, "Cat, is the ring all right?"

The cat was so angry that the dog did not trust her, that she yowled, "Of course the ring is all right!" But as soon as she opened her mouth, the ring fell into the river.

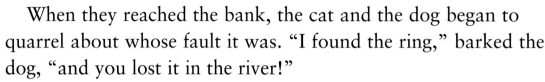

When they reached the bank, the cat and the dog began to quarrel about whose fault it was. "I found the ring," barked the dog, "and you lost it in the river!"

The cat yowled, "If you had trusted me, you would not have asked about the ring. Then I would not have dropped it!" The dog barked and started chasing the cat. Finally, the cat ran up a tree and stayed there all night, while the dog walked sadly home to Taro and Kita.

In the morning, the cat saw a fisherman catching fish near the place in the river where she had dropped the ring. She climbed down from her tree and slowly crept up behind the fisherman. *Oh*, she thought to herself, *if I could take a fish home to Taro and Kita, we would all have something to eat.* While the fisherman was busy with his nets, the cat grabbed a fish from his pile and carried it home.

Taro and Kita were happy to see the cat. Kita said, "Ah, little cat, you have brought us something to eat!" When Kita cut open the fish to cook it, there lay the magic ring! "Ah," said Taro, "our good fortune has returned!"

Kita and Taro praised the cat for returning the ring. But the dog was jealous. He again barked at the cat, "No one knows that I found the ring, because you dropped it in the river."

The cat yowled as she scratched at the dog, "If you had only trusted me, I would never have dropped it."

So to this day, the dog and the cat are still arguing!

 TRUST IS AN IMPORTANT PART OF FRIENDSHIP

Source notes

All My Shining Silver
Donegal Fairy Stories by Seumas MacManus
(Doubleday, 1900)

Hadiyah and the Great Fish
Kings, Gods & Spirits from African Mythology by Jan Knappert
(Peter Bendrick Books, 1986)

Awang and the Silver Flute
Kantchil's Lime Pit and other Stories from Indonesia by Harold
Courlander (Harcourt, Brace & World, 1950)

The Danced-Out Shoes
Russian Fairy Tales, edited and translated by Norbert Guterman
(Pantheon, 1945)

The Rainbow Horse
The Rainbow-Colored Horse, by Pura Belpré,
(Frederick Warne, 1978)

Why Dog and Cat are Not Friends
"The Monkey, the Cat, and the Rat," in *Japanese Folk Tales* by Kunio
Yanagita, (Orient Cultural Service, 1972): *Korean Folk & Fairy Tales*,
retold by Suzanne Crowder Han, (HollyM International, 1991).